Sleeping Beauty
& The Frog Prince

Best-Loved Fairy Tales
Illustrated by Anastassija Archipowa
Retold by Jane Resnick

DERRYDALE BOOKS

New York

Sleeping Beauty

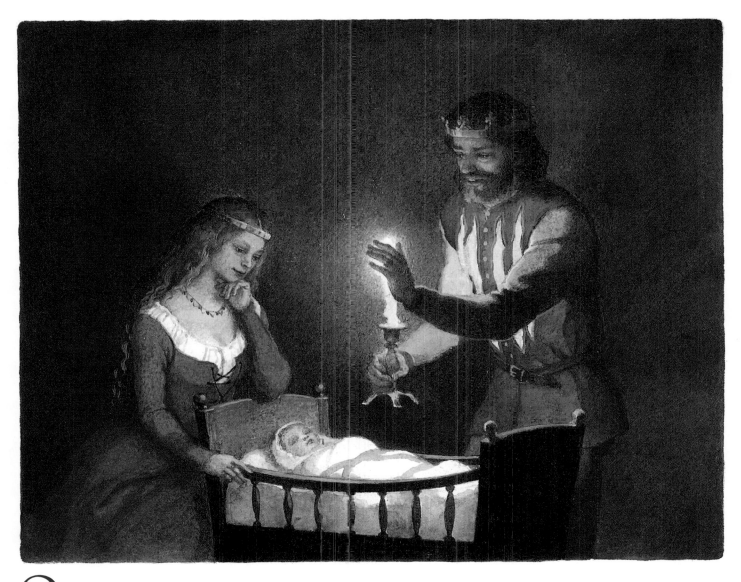

Once there lived a King and Queen who longed for a child, but they had none. At last, the Queen gave birth to a baby girl. She was so charming that the King could not contain his joy.

He decided to hold a great celebration and invite all the Wise Women of the kingdom — all except one, for there were thirteen Wise Women and only twelve golden plates. At the end of the feast, each one gave a magic gift to the tiny Princess. One gave the Princess beauty, another, virtue, a third, wisdom.

But before the last had spoken, the Wise Woman who had not been invited burst into the room. Furious at being neglected, she brought a curse instead of a blessing.

Bitterly, she called out, "When the Princess is fifteen, she will prick her finger on a spindle and die!" She stormed out without uttering another word.

But then the twelfth Wise Woman stepped forward, for she

had not yet given her gift.

"I cannot lift the curse," she said, "but I can alter it. The Princess will not die. She will fall into a deep sleep, which will last one hundred years. Then she will be awakened by a King's son."

Grief-stricken, the King vowed to protect his child. He ordered that every spindle in the kingdom be destroyed.

As time passed, all the Wise Women's blessings were fulfilled. The Princess grew to be beautiful, kind, sweet-natured and wise, and all who knew her loved her.

On her fifteenth birthday, it so happened that the inquisitive princess was wandering through the great castle exploring. High in a tower, she discovered a strange room, where there sat an old woman busily spinning wool. The Princess, who had never seen this before, was very curious.

"What are you doing?" she asked.

"Spinning," said the woman.

"May I try?" asked the girl.

Yet as soon as she took the spindle into her hand, she pricked her finger, and the wicked curse came true. The Princess fell upon a bed in the

room and a deep sleep came over her. Suddenly, everyone else in the castle fell asleep, too.

The King and Queen fell asleep on their thrones and the people of their court fell asleep wherever they were. The horses went to sleep in the stables, the dogs in the yard, the pigeons on the roof, and the flies on the wall. Even the fire in the hearth flickered and then stopped burning. The meat that was roasting went cold.

And the cook, who was about to pull the kitchen boy's hair because he had done something wrong, let him go and fell asleep with a great snore. The kitchen boy fell asleep, too. The breeze stopped blowing, and not a leaf stirred in the trees in front of the palace. Everything in the castle was silent.

All around the castle a thorny briar hedge began to grow where there had once been fields of beautiful flowers. Every year the hedge grew higher and thicker until it surrounded and hid the palace, so that nothing could be seen, not even the flag that flew from the roof of the highest tower, now standing still.

But the castle and its inhabitants were not forgotten. The story of the beautiful sleeping Princess was told far and wide and became a legend throughout the land. Over the years, many princes came and tried to force their way through the briar bushes to the palace. But none succeeded. They were cut by the thorns of the briar bushes and forced to turn away.

After many, many years a Prince came to the country

and heard an old man tell the story of the castle behind the briar hedge. He described the beautiful Princess who lay sleeping there with the King and Queen and all their court. The old man also knew from his father that many princes had tried to force themselves through the fierce briar hedge, only to fail.

But the young Prince said, "I am not afraid. I must see the lovely sleeping Princess."

The old man tried to dissuade him, but the Prince would not listen.

Now it so happened that the hundred years had passed and the day had come for the Princess to awaken. When the Prince approached the briar hedge, the briars blossomed into flowers. A path through the hedge opened for him, and he passed through unharmed.

In the courtyard he saw the horses and dogs lying asleep. On the roof the pigeons were curled up with their heads beneath their wings.

When he entered the castle it seemed haunted with a ghostly silence. The people of the court

were asleep in the great hall, and the King and Queen were asleep on their thrones. The Prince searched the palace. At last he came to the tower where the Princess lay sleeping. She was so beautiful that he bent down and gently kissed her. At the touch of his lips, the Princess opened her eyes and smiled sweetly.

Then they went down from the tower together. As they descended, the King and Queen and the whole court woke up and looked at each other in wonder. The horses and dogs and pigeons and flies came to life. The fire began crackling, and the meat resumed roasting. The cook pulled the kitchen boy's hair, and all returned to normal.

Then the wedding of the Prince and the Princess was celebrated in splendor. They lived happily in the castle until the end of their days.

The Frog Prince

Once there lived a king whose youngest daughter was so lovely that the dazzling sun was amazed at her beauty. The beautiful princess often played in the forest, throwing her favorite golden ball into the air and catching it.

Now it happened one day that the golden ball did not fall back into the maiden's hand. When she threw it aloft, it dropped to the ground and bounced into a nearby well. The princess watched in horror as the golden ball sank into the well until she could no longer see it. Then she began to weep bitterly.

Through her sobs, the princess heard someone call out to her, "What is the matter, Princess? Your sad tears would melt the heart of a stone."

When the princess looked up, all she saw was the ugly head of a frog sticking out of the water.

"Oh, it is only you, old water splasher," she said. "I am weeping because my favorite toy, my golden ball, has fallen into the well."

"Do not weep," said the frog. "I can help you. But what will you give me if I bring back your favorite plaything?"

"Whatever you like, dear frog," she said. "My clothes, my jewels and pearls, even my golden crown."

"Your clothes, your jewels and pearls, and your golden crown are all useless to me," answered the frog. "But if you would love me, if you would let me be your companion, and sit at your table, and eat from your plate, and drink from your cup, and put my head on your pillow....If you promise all this, I would dive to the bottom of the well and fetch your golden ball."

"I will promise whatever you want," she answered, "if only you will bring me my ball." But the princess thought to herself. "What nonsense! This frog can only sit in the water and croak with the other frogs. He cannot be anyone's companion!"

The moment the frog heard her promise, he dove into the water. After a few moments he came swimming back to the surface with her golden ball. Thrilled to see her lovely plaything, the princess picked up the ball and ran off.

"Wait!" cried the frog. "Take me too. I cannot keep up with you!" He croaked and croaked at the top of his lungs, but it did him no good.

The next day the princess was at the supper table with the king and his court when there was a knock at the door. The princess ran to see who it was, but when she opened the door, there was the frog! Frightened, she shut the door and ran back to the table.

"What is the matter?" the king asked. "Who was at the door?"

"No one," she replied, "Just a horrible frog."

"What does the frog want?" asked the king.

"Oh, Father," the princess tearfully replied, "yesterday I was playing in the forest with my golden ball. It fell deep into a well, and because I wept so hard, a frog fetched it up for me. In return, I promised the frog that it could be my companion, but I never thought the frog could leave the well. And now it is at the door! The horrible creature wants to come in."

Then the frog knocked at the door a second time and called, "Princess! Let me in. Let your promise of yesterday be true today."

The king said to his daughter,

"When you make a promise, you must keep it."

So the princess opened the door. The frog hopped in and sat on the table. He ate from the princess' golden plate and drank from the princess' golden cup. Disgusted, she begged the frog to leave, but he would not.

Then the frog said, "I am very tired. Carry me upstairs so that I may rest my head on your soft, fluffy pillow."

The princess began to cry, for she was afraid of the cold frog and hated to touch him.

Now the king grew angry and said, "He helped you, my dear, and you must keep your promise!"

So the princess picked up the frog, carried him upstairs and put him down in a corner. But the frog came hopping over and said, "Pick me up so I can put my head on your pillow."

Furious, she picked him up and threw him across the room,

crying, "Now you will be quiet, you horrid frog!"

But when he hit the floor, he was no longer a frog. He became a handsome prince!

The prince told her how a wicked witch had cast a spell on him and how no one but she alone could have freed him. And so with her father's consent, they became bride and bridegroom. The next day, the prince told her, they would go together to live in his father's kingdom.

And as soon as the sun rose, a magnificent carriage arrived. It was drawn by eight white horses, fastened with golden harnesses and crowned with plumes of white feathers. The carriage was driven by the prince's faithful servant, Henry.

Faithful Henry had been so distressed when his master was turned into a horrid frog that he had the blacksmith forge three

iron bands around his heart to keep it from bursting with grief and sadness.

When Henry received word that he was to bring the prince home, he was filled with hope that the spell might be broken. When he at last saw the handsome prince, standing with a beautiful princess, his heart was bursting with joy. He lifted the prince and princess into the carriage and took his seat in the back, delighted that his master had been set free.

The prince and princess sat together lovingly, marveling at the happiness they had found so unexpectedly. Suddenly, their peaceful union was broken by a cracking sound at the back of the carriage. It seemed as if something had broken. Alarmed, the prince turned around and cried, "Henry, what was that sound? The wheel must

be breaking off the carriage!"

But Henry answered, "No, master, do not fear. That sound is the breaking of the bands around my heart. Since you are a frog no more, my heart swells with gladness. The sound of the breaking marks the end of my sadness."

Again and then again the prince heard the same cracking sound — three times in all. And each time he thought the carriage must be breaking to pieces. But it was only the sound of the iron bands breaking away from Faithful Henry's heart, because he was so filled with joy.